Spider Dan

This book is dedicated to:
All picky eaters and Maria and James - Norman
My love bugs Melissa, CJ, and Morgan. Thank you Vickey
for your guidance, skill, and most of all – friendship. - Charlie

Text copyright © 1997 by Norman B. Foote
Based on the song "Spider Dan" lyrics and music by Norman B. Foote
© Branch Group Music Publishing and Footever Music
Illustrations copyright © 1997 by Charlie Mitchell

Whitecap Books
Vancouver/Toronto
Published by arrangement with
LONGSTREET PRESS, INC.
A subsidiary of Cox Newspapers,
A subsidiary of Cox Enterprises, Inc.
2140 Newmarket Parkway, Suite 122
Marietta, Georgia 30067

Produced by Vickey Bolling
Printed by Paramount Printing Company Limited, Hong Kong
The text of this book is set in 16 point Stone Informal. The illustrations are in acrylics,
gouache and coloring pencil on Strathmore illustration board.

1st Printing, 1997
Canadian Cataloguing in Publication Data
Foote, Norman.
Spider Dan
ISBN 1-55110-652-3
1. Spiders–Juvenile fiction. 2. Frogs–Juvenile fiction. I. Mitchell, Charlie. II. Title.
PS8561.O6316S64 1997   jC813'.54   C97-910383-5
PZ7.F747Sp 1997

Special thanks to Gilles Paquin and the Oak Street Music label. For more information, contact Oak Street at Paquin@magic.mb.ca.

Spider Dan

Written by Norman B. Foote • Illustrated by Charlie Mitchell

"Now Spider Dan," said his spider mother,
"I'll tell you what I've told your brothers.
You must go out and learn to survive,
By trapping food to stay alive."

"Spiders eat bugs, like mosquitoes or flies;
Fuzzy little things that fly in the sky."

"We spin a web – that's where they stick."
But the mere thought of this made Dan feel sick!

So Dan went out in his back yard,
And spun a web – it wasn't *that* hard.
He waited till dark and he stood nearby;
Then along came Beatrice, the butterfly.

She flew to and fro like butterflies do,
Till she hit Dan's web and she stuck like glue.

She yelled, "Help me! I'm too young to die!
Give me a break — I just learned how to fly!
Come on, Mister Spider, it's far too soon;
I just got out of my cocoon!
I'm just getting used to my brand-new wings.
Look at me, I'm just an iddy-biddy thing!"

Dan shook his head, "I just don't know.
I can't eat that — Oh no, Oh no!
Butterfly, I'll let you go!"

Soon there was a noise out back;
It was a cockroach in tuxedo and hat.
He yelled, "I should have stayed in bed.
Help me! It's Henry — I'm stuck in a web!"

Then Dan exclaimed, "It's dinner at last!"
Henry moaned, "Help me. Do something fast!
Please Mister Spider, leave me alone.
I've got thirty-two kids and a wife at home!"

Dan shook his head, "I just don't know.
I can't eat that — Oh no, Oh no!
Okay, Cockroach, I'll let you go!"

But just as soon as the coast was clear,
A mosquito named Merv came buzzing near.

He didn't see what lay ahead,
And he flew straight into that spider's web.

He said, "Wait a minute — you can't eat me.
Take a good look; I'm as skinny as can be.
I know this may sound outrageous,
But I've got a flu bug and I'm contagious!"

Dan shook his head, "I just don't know.
I can't eat that — Oh no, Oh no!
Okay, Mosquito, I'll let you go!"

Just when Dan had hidden from sight,
A GREAT, **big** frog jumped out of the night.

Dan said, "What's this? It's not a bug.
It could ruin my web with a single tug."

But the frog saw Dan
And with a flick of her tongue. . .

She gobbled him up,
And the frog said *"Yummm."*

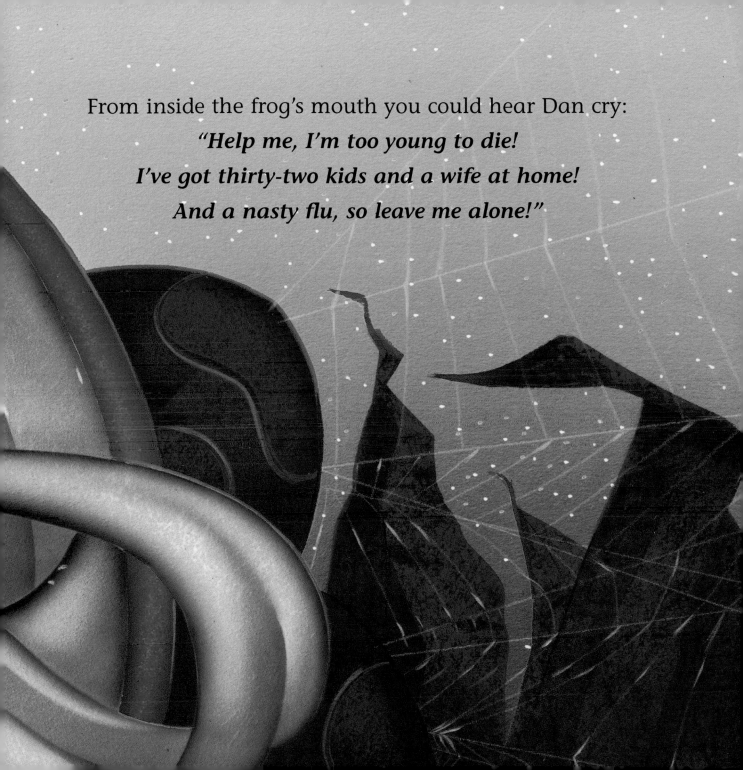

From inside the frog's mouth you could hear Dan cry:

"Help me, I'm too young to die!

I've got thirty-two kids and a wife at home!

And a nasty flu, so leave me alone!"

Just when poor Dan had lost all hope,
The frog began to gag and choke;
And with a coughing, gasping sound,
She spat Dan out upon the ground.

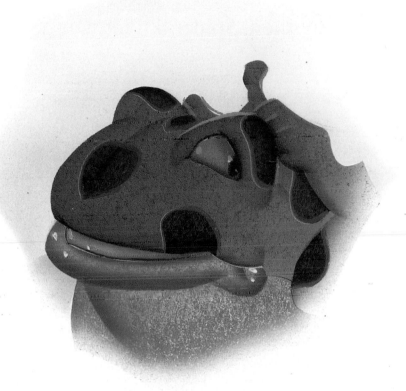

AND DO YOU KNOW WHAT THAT FROG DID NEXT?

(Go ahead and try to guess.)

She shook her head. "I just don't know.
I can't eat that — Oh no, Oh no!
Okay then, Spider, I'll let you go!"

"Now that was close," Dan said, "but wait!
We could be friends. It's not too late.
Let's go get something good to eat."

"Like melon rinds or crumbs of bread.
Now *that* would be a treat!"